LITTLE WOMEN

Louisa May Alcott

LEVEL 1

D1421043

Adapted by: Jane Revell

Publisher: Jacquie Bloese

Editor: Emma Grisewood

Designer: Christine Cox

Picture research: Pupak Navabpour

Photo credits:
Cover and inside images © 1994 Columbia Pictures Industries, Inc.
All Rights Reserved. Courtesy of Columbia Pictures.
Cover: Ailime, nicolay/iStockphoto
Pages 4, 5, 7, 8, 48, 49, 50, 51, 52 & 53: Ailime/iStockphoto.
Pages 16, 18, 23 & 29: nicolay/iStockphoto.
Pages 48 & 49: The Granger Collection/Topfoto; Mary Evans
Picture Library.
Pages 50 & 51: Mary Evans Picture Library; North Wind Pictures
Archive/Alamy.
Pages 52 & 53: Mary Evans Picture Library

Illustrations (pages 6 & 7): Doreen Lang

Contents

THE MARCH FAMILY

MRS MARCH is the mother of four daughters. The girls call their mother 'Marmee'.

MEG (Margaret) is the oldest daughter. She is sixteen. She loves nice clothes and she likes to look pretty.

JO (Josephine) is fifteen. She loves reading and writing stories. She doesn't care about clothes and pretty things.

Twelve-year-old **AMY** is the youngest sister. She is very pretty. Amy thinks more about Amy than about other people.

MR MARCH is away from home at war. Life is difficult for the family.

BETH is thirteen. She is a quiet, shy girl. Sometimes she is frightened of people but she loves her sisters.

AUNT MARCH is old and very rich.

HANNAH lives with the family and helps them.

THE LAURENCES

LAURIE (Theodore Laurence) lives in the big house next to the Marches' house with his grandfather MR James LAURENCE.

MR John BROOKE is Laurie's tutor.

PLACES

Massachusetts

Washington

The story starts in the early 1860s, in Massachusetts in America. It is the time of the American Civil War.

MASSACHUSETTS is a state in America. **WASHINGTON** is the capital of America.

Useful words in the 1860s

ice-cream
People liked to eat ice-cream at parties. It was special!

basket
Ladies took their things everywhere in a basket. At home, young ladies had their sewing things in a basket.

gloves
Young ladies always had gloves at parties.

handkerchief
Young ladies always had a handkerchief with them.

sash
Ladies had sashes on their party dresses.

fan
Ladies used a fan to stay cool at parties.

carriage
Rich people went from place to place in carriages like this.

telegram
People didn't have telephones or email. The quickest way to tell important news was by telegram.

People didn't have television or computers. What did they do in the evenings?

drawing (draw / drew)

painting

sewing

playing the piano

The language of Louisa May Alcott's time

Louisa May Alcott was an American writer. She wrote *Little Women* in 1868. That was almost 150 years ago!

A lot of things were different then. A lot of words were different too. Here are some of the words you can find in *Little Women*.

THEN		NOW
*governess / tutor**	=	*teacher*
drawing room / parlour	=	*living room*
wonderful	=	*great / fantastic*

People only used first names for children, families and very good friends. Meg calls John Brooke *Mr Brooke*. Young people called older men *Sir* and older women *Ma'am*.

Children called their mum *Mother* and their dad *Father*.

* In those days, some rich children didn't go to school. They had their lessons at home with a governess (woman) or a tutor (man).

LITTLE WOMEN

CHAPTER 1
The four sisters

'No Christmas presents this year,' said Jo sadly. She was on the floor in front of the fire in the drawing room.

'I hate being poor,' said Meg. She looked at her old dress.

'Some girls have lots of pretty things. Other girls don't have anything,' said Amy. 'It's not right.'

'We've got Father and Mother,' said Beth happily. 'And we've each got three sisters!'

All the girls smiled for a moment.

They were all good friends. The older girls helped the younger ones. Meg was very close to Amy. Jo and Beth were very different. Jo was loud and Beth was quiet, but they were very close too.

'We haven't got Father,' Jo said. 'He's going to be away for a long time.'

'Mother thinks it's wrong to buy presents when there's a war,' said Meg. 'But I want lots of pretty things to wear.'

'Well, we've each got a little money,' said Jo. 'We can each buy one present. I'm going to buy a book.'

Beth loved to play the piano. 'I'd like some music,' she said.

'I'm going to buy some drawing pencils,' said Amy. Amy was very good at drawing.

'I think it's OK to buy one present,' said Jo. 'We work a lot.'

'I know I work a lot,' said Meg, 'and those children are terrible.' Meg was a governess for a rich family.

'I work more than you,' said Jo. 'I'm alone with Aunt March for hours. She's a difficult old woman.'

'I hate washing clothes and cleaning the house,' said Beth quietly.

'I have the worst time,' cried Amy. 'I go to school every day and the rich girls laugh at me. I hate it.'

Jo sat up and started to whistle.

'Don't whistle, Jo,' said Amy. 'Boys do that! Ladies don't whistle!'

'That's why I do it,' said Jo.

Everyone laughed.

* * *

'It's six o'clock,' said Beth. 'Marmee's going to be here soon.'

Jo took her mother's shoes and warmed them in front of the fire. 'These shoes are very old,' she said. 'She needs some new ones.'

'I can buy her some with my money,' said Beth.

'No, I can,' shouted Amy.

'No, I'm the oldest,' cried Meg.

'No, I'm the man of the family now,' said Jo.

'I know,' said Beth. 'Let's each buy her something. We don't need Christmas presents.'

'Oh, Beth, you're so kind,' said Jo. 'What is everyone going to buy?'

'I'm going to give her gloves,' said Meg.

'And I'm going to make her some pretty handkerchiefs,' said Beth.

'I can buy her some perfume,' said Amy. 'It isn't expensive. I can still buy my drawing pencils.'

There was a happy 'Hello!' from the door. Marmee arrived in her grey coat and old hat. 'How are you all?' she cried.

The girls ran to help. Beth took Marmee's coat and hat, Jo gave her warm shoes, and Meg put things on the tea table.

Marmee said: 'I've got a surprise for you!'

The girls smiled. 'A letter from father!' they cried.

'Yes, a long letter,' said their mother.

They all sat near the fire and Marmee read the letter. At the end of the letter their father wrote: *Tell the girls that I think of them. A year is a long time. But I know my little women are good and strong.*

When they heard that, all the girls cried a little. They wanted their father to be happy. They decided to try to be good and strong.

After tea, they took out their sewing baskets and sewed happily together. Later, at nine, they stopped and stood around the old piano. They did this every evening. Beth played and everyone sang.

Marmee sang too. She sang beautifully. She sang every day when she got up. It was the first thing that the girls heard every morning.

CHAPTER 2
A happy Christmas

The next morning was Christmas Day. There was no sound of singing when the girls woke up. Meg and Jo ran down to the living room.

'Where's Mother?' they asked Hannah. Hannah lived with the family and helped them.

'She went to see someone,' said Hannah.

Meg looked at the basket near the sofa. In it, there were the presents for Marmee.

'Where's Amy's perfume?' she asked.

'Amy took it a few minutes ago,' Jo said. 'I don't know why.'

Suddenly Amy came in. She had her coat and hat on.

'Where were you, Amy?' asked Meg.

'I went to the shop to change my present for Marmee,' said Amy. 'I gave them my cheap perfume and bought a big, expensive one. I used all my money so now I can't buy any drawing pencils. I'm trying to be good.'

Meg put her arms around Amy.

Then the door opened again and Marmee was there.

'Happy Christmas, Marmee!' they cried.

'Happy Christmas, little daughters!' She smiled at them all. 'Now, I must ask you something. A very poor woman, Mrs Hummel, lives not far away. She has six children. They have no fire and nothing to eat. And they are very, very hungry. Can we give them our breakfast for a Christmas present?'

The girls were very hungry. No one said a word for a moment. Jo looked at her sisters and then said, 'Of course!'

'Thank you, girls,' said Marmee.

The sisters put the breakfast in their baskets. They walked through the streets with bread, cakes and tea.

When they arrived at the poor little house, the children looked at them sadly with their big eyes. Hannah made a fire, Mrs March gave the mother some tea and the girls put the food on the table.

'You are very good people!' cried Mrs Hummel. 'Thank you.'

* * *

The girls loved acting. Jo wrote exciting plays for them to act. This Christmas, it was a love story between beautiful Zara and good-looking Rodrigo. But terrible Hugo wanted Zara too. He asked Hagar to help him. Hugo hated Rodrigo. Rodrigo must die!

Jo was Hugo. She was always the bad man! Amy was beautiful Zara and Meg was Hagar. It was a wonderful play. Everyone enjoyed it. At the end, Marmee came into their room.

'Thank you for my lovely presents, girls,' she said. 'Now I have a surprise for you, too. Come down for tea.'

'Tea?' the girls cried as they ran down.

When they saw the table, their mouths fell open with surprise. There was cake and fruit and pink ice-cream and white ice-cream ... and lots of lovely things to eat and drink.

'Is it Father Christmas?' asked Beth.

'Is it Aunt March?' asked Jo.

'No, it's old Mr Laurence and his grandson in the big house next to ours,' said their mother. 'He heard about your breakfast. This is his Christmas present. Happy Christmas, girls!'

CHAPTER 3
The party

'Jo! Jo! Where are you?' called Meg.

'Here!' answered Jo.

Meg ran up to the top of the house. Jo was in her favourite place by the window ... with a book.

'Look!' cried Meg. She had a paper in her hand. 'It's from Mrs Gardiner. She's having a New Year party tomorrow night. She wants us to go! What can we wear?'

'Well, that's not a problem,' said Jo. 'You've only got one dress. Me too.' She thought for a minute. 'But my dress has a big hole in the back.'

'Then you must sit all evening,' said Meg, 'with your back to the wall.'

'My gloves have got holes in, too,' said Jo. 'I can't wear them.'

'No gloves?' cried Meg. 'Gloves are so important, Jo. You must have gloves! I can't go with you if you haven't!'

'I've got an idea,' Jo said. 'Give me one of your gloves. Then we can each wear one good glove. We can have a bad glove in the other hand.'

* * *

At last, Meg and Jo were ready. They walked out of the house and across the garden.

'Have a good time, girls!' Mrs March called after them. 'Have you got nice handkerchiefs?'

'Yes,' cried the girls and they laughed. Marmee always asked that question when they went out.

Meg and Jo didn't go to parties often. They were a little

shy. At the party, they met Mrs Gardiner's daughter, Sallie. Sallie's friend, Annie Moffat, was there too. Meg, Sallie and Annie talked about clothes and fashion. It was boring for Jo. She stood with her back against the wall and watched a group of boys. She heard the word 'skating'. Now *that* was interesting. Jo loved skating. She wanted to talk to the boys. A young man with red hair walked across the room.

'Help! He's coming to ask me to dance!' Jo thought. She quickly moved into a little room. She wanted to be alone.

She looked around. She wasn't alone. There was a boy in the room.

'Oh, I'm sorry,' said Jo. 'I didn't know ...' She started to go out again.

The boy laughed. 'That's all right,' he said. 'Please stay.'

'I think I know you,' said Jo. 'Don't you live near us?'

'Next to you,' said the boy. He and Jo both laughed.

'Thank you for your nice Christmas present, Mr Laurence,' Jo said.

'My grandfather gave it to you, Miss March,' said the boy.

'I'm not Miss March. I'm only Jo,' said Jo.

'And I'm not Mr Laurence,' said the boy. 'I'm only Laurie. My name's Theodore but I don't like it. So I'm Laurie.'

'I hate my name too,' said Jo. 'Josephine! Ugh! Do you like parties?'

'Sometimes,' said Laurie, 'but I don't know many people here. I lived in Europe for many years ...'

'Oh! Tell me about it!' cried Jo. 'I love listening to stories about different countries.'

So Laurie talked about Paris and Germany and Italy. And Jo asked lots of questions. They talked and laughed and watched the other people at the party.

Later in the evening Meg came to find Jo. Jo saw she had a problem with her foot.

'Oh, Meg! What's wrong?' asked Jo.

'It's these stupid shoes! I don't usually wear them,' said Meg. 'I danced all evening and now I can't walk!'

'You need a carriage to go home,' said Jo.

'No!' said Meg. 'Carriages are expensive! We can wait here for Hannah. I can walk with her help.'

Laurie went away. He came back with a coffee for Meg and some ice for her foot.

'My carriage is here,' he said. 'I'm going to take you both home.'

When they were in the carriage Jo asked her sister: 'Did you have a good time?'

'Yes, I did,' said Meg. 'Annie Moffat asked Sallie Gardiner to stay with her family for a week in the spring. She asked me too. Isn't that exciting?'

CHAPTER 4
Problems

When Mr March had money problems, his daughters wanted to help. Meg found a job as a governess and Jo worked for her rich Aunt March. The morning after the party, they went back to work. The holidays were finished. The girls weren't happy at breakfast that morning.

'It's nice to go to parties and drive home in a carriage,' said Meg. 'I don't want to work.'

'I didn't do my homework,' said Amy, 'And now I can't find my school things.'

'I'm tired,' said Beth. Beth didn't often talk about her problems.

Jo just whistled and said, 'I'm sorry it isn't Christmas every day!'

After breakfast, Meg and Jo put on their hats and coats.

'Bye, Marmee!' they said. 'We're sorry we're not very nice this morning. Play with your cats, Beth, to help you feel better.'

They went out of the door to start their long walk. At the end of the garden they turned. Their mother was always in the window. She always smiled at them.

'I hate being poor and I hate working,' said Meg. 'I want to stay at home like other girls. I want to have nice things.'

'When I'm rich, you can have carriages and ice-cream and beautiful shoes,' said Jo.

Meg laughed. They said goodbye and went their different ways.

Meg worked for the King family. They were very rich. Their children were spoilt and difficult. It wasn't easy for Meg. Every day she saw their nice things and pretty clothes. She remembered happier days for her family. They had nice things and pretty clothes then too.

Old Aunt March was very rich. She had no children. She needed someone to help her. Jo talked to her and read to her. She didn't enjoy it but she loved one thing. She loved Aunt March's books! Sometimes Aunt March went to sleep. Then Jo was very happy. She ran to the room with lots of books. She sat in a big chair and read. She never read for very long. Aunt March always woke up and called her: 'Josy-phine! Josy-phine!' She put down her book and went back to her aunt.

Beth didn't go to school. She was too frightened of people. Before the war, she learned her lessons with her father at home. When he went away, she did her lessons alone. Beth helped Hannah too. She cleaned the house and helped in the kitchen. She was always busy. She liked to make the house nice for her mother and sisters. And she played with her cats. But Beth loved music most. She played the old piano every day. She needed lessons, but it wasn't possible. Sometimes she was sad about that and she cried quietly.

Amy's biggest problem was her nose. She didn't like it. She tried to change it. She pulled it with her fingers but it stayed the same. She was very good at drawing so her sisters called her 'Little Raphael'*. She knew some French too and she had a lot of friends at school. But Amy was the youngest daughter. She was a bit spoilt and she didn't always think about other people.

That evening, the girls worked at their sewing. They talked sadly about their day.

'Tell us a story, Marmee,' said Jo.

Mrs March smiled. She told her daughters a story about four girls. These four girls had lovely parents and friends. They each had three sisters. They lived in a nice house. They had enough to eat and drink. But they always wanted more things. They weren't happy. One day they asked an old woman, 'How can we be happy?'

The old woman said, 'You have lots of things. When you feel sad, think about all those things. And be happy.'

The girls did that, and they were surprised. It worked.

'You're very clever, Marmee!' cried Meg.

'I like that story,' said Beth.

'I'm going to try to be happier,' Amy said.

And Jo just said, 'We needed that lesson, Marmee. Thank you.'

* Raphael (1483-1520) was a famous Italian painter.

CHAPTER 5
Making friends

One afternoon, Jo was in their little garden. It was white with snow. Jo loved to be out in the snow. She looked at the Laurence's big garden next to theirs. The Laurence's house was very big too. Jo looked up at it. She was surprised to see Laurie. He was looking out of a window at the top of the house.

'How are you, Laurie?' she called.

Laurie opened the window. 'I was ill,' he shouted. 'I'm almost better now … but I can't go out …'

'Do you want me to come and talk to you?' asked Jo.

'Yes, please. My grandfather isn't here at the moment,' said Laurie. Jo was happy. She was a bit frightened of old Mr Laurence.

'I must ask my mother,' she said.

A little later, Jo was in Laurie's parlour. She had some ice-cream in one hand and a basket with three cats in the other.

'Ice-cream is easy to eat,' she said. 'It's from Meg. The cats are from Beth.'

Laurie laughed. 'I feel better already,' he said. 'Sometimes I feel very alone. Thank you for coming.'

'You can come to our house too,' said Jo.

She sat down and they talked and laughed for a long time.

Later in the afternoon, the doctor arrived. Jo went into the big drawing room and waited. She looked at a big picture of Mr Laurence, Laurie's grandfather.

'You've got nice eyes,' she said to the picture. 'I'm not frightened of you now. I like you.'

'I'm happy to hear that,' someone said behind her. It was old Mr Laurence. Jo's face was very red. 'Did you come to see my grandson?' he asked.

'Yes,' she said. 'He's alone a lot. I think he's happy to talk to someone.'

'Well, come and have some tea with us,' said Mr Laurence.

Jo, Laurie and Mr Laurence sat in front of the fire in the big drawing room. There was a beautiful piano in the room.

'Please can you play something?' Jo asked Laurie.

So Laurie played and Jo listened. He played very well. 'I must tell Beth,' she thought.

When Laurie was better, he often came to the March's house. Life was much more fun there! He played games with the girls; they went walking and skating; they acted in Jo's stories; they had parties.

The girls went to the big house too. Meg enjoyed the garden. Amy looked at the pictures and did drawings. Jo read lots of books. Only Beth didn't go. She was shy.

Mr Laurence knew this. One day he said to Mrs March, 'No one plays our piano now. It's very sad. Do your girls want to play it? Please ask them.'

When Beth heard this, she said, 'I want to play it, Sir. I love to play. I'm Beth.'

'Then come when you want, Beth,' said Mr Laurence.

And almost every day after that, Beth went to the Laurence's house. She sat in the great drawing room and played the piano for hours. And often Mr Laurence opened the door of his room to listen.

CHAPTER 6
A terrible thing to do

Meg and Jo had their hats and coats on.

'Where are you going?' Amy asked them.

'We're not going to tell you,' said Jo.

'Are you going somewhere with Laurie?'

'Yes, now please be quiet.'

'I know! I know! You're going to see 'The Seven Castles'*. I want to come too.'

'Well, you can't,' said Jo. 'It's not for little girls.'

'You were ill last week, Amy,' said Meg nicely. 'You can't go out yet.'

'Oh, please!' cried Amy. 'Please!' She started to put on her hat.

'No, Amy,' said Jo. 'You can't come. So stop asking! Oh ... there's Laurie. Let's go.'

As Meg and Jo went out, Amy called out, 'You're going to be sorry for this, Jo March!'

* 'The Seven Castles' is a play.

When they arrived home again, Amy was in the parlour with a book. She didn't say a word.

'Maybe everything is all right,' thought Jo.

But it wasn't.

Jo didn't only write stories. She wanted to write a book. She hoped to finish it before their father came home.

The next day, she ran into the parlour and cried, 'Where's my book?'

Meg and Beth looked surprised. Amy said nothing but her face was red.

'Amy, you've got it.'

'No, I haven't.'

'That's not true!'

'It is true. I haven't got it. But you're not going to see your stupid old book again.'

'Why not?'

'I put in on the fire.'

'What? My lovely book? I worked on that book for months! You put it on the fire?'

'Yes. I did. You weren't nice to me yesterday. I told you ...'

Amy didn't finish. Jo shouted at her. 'That's a terrible thing to do! You're a bad, bad girl! I can never write it again. I hate you!' She ran out of the room.

Mrs March came home. Meg and Beth told her the story. Marmee talked to Amy. When Jo came down for tea, Amy said, 'I'm very, very sorry, Jo. Please don't hate me.'

'I'm never going to speak to you again,' said Jo.

Later Marmee said to Jo quietly, 'Don't go to bed angry, Jo. Be nice to Amy. Start again tomorrow.'

'I can't, Marmee,' Jo said. 'It was a terrible thing to do.'

The next day, Jo and Laurie went skating. Amy saw them leave.

'I want to go with them,' she said to Meg. 'But Jo doesn't want me.'

'Go after them,' said Meg. 'Jo's happy when she's skating. It's a good time to talk to her.'

So Amy followed Jo and Laurie to the river. Jo saw her but she didn't say anything.

'Why is she following me? I hate her,' she thought. Laurie skated first to test the ice.

He shouted to Jo. 'Don't go in the centre. The ice isn't strong. You can fall through!'

Jo heard him but Amy didn't hear. Jo didn't care. Jo skated after Laurie.

Amy skated across the river. Suddenly, Jo heard a loud cry. She turned and saw Amy. Amy was in the icy water. Amy's head went under the water.

Jo was very frightened. She called out to Laurie. Laurie was with Amy in a minute. He carefully pulled her out of the water. Amy was very cold and frightened. She cried.

'We must warm her and take her home quickly,' said Laurie.

Laurie put his coat around Amy. Together Jo and Laurie took Amy home. Marmee put her in front of the fire. When she was warm again, she went to sleep.

'Is she going to be all right?' Jo asked Marmee.

'Yes,' said Marmee. 'You helped her very quickly.'

'Laurie did,' said Jo. She started to cry. 'Oh Marmee, I saw her behind me but I didn't say anything. I was still so angry with her because of my book. I know it's wrong. How can I change? Help me.'

'Learn to say nothing when you are angry, Jo,' said her mother. 'I am sometimes very angry too. I think for a minute and then I feel better.'

'But you're never angry, mother,' said Jo.

'Yes, I am, Jo. When I was a girl, I was often angry, too,' said Marmee. 'I tried to change.'

'I'm going to try too, Marmee,' said Jo.

She went over to Amy and put her arms around her. Amy opened her eyes and smiled up at her sister. The girls were friends again.

CHAPTER 7
Meg goes to the Moffats

One day in April, a letter arrived from Annie Moffat.

'She remembered!' cried Meg. 'Sallie Gardiner and I are going to stay with the Moffats. For two weeks!'

Her sisters helped Meg. Jo helped with her skirts. Amy helped with her sewing things. Marmee gave her some special things: a fan and a beautiful sash.

The next day, Meg left. Mrs March wasn't very happy. The Moffats were rich people. They were very different from the March family. They thought different things were important. 'I hope Meg doesn't change when she's there,' she thought.

The Moffats lived in a very big house. They had lots of beautiful things. Every day the girls went for a walk or a drive in the carriage. They went shopping and they went to see friends. In the evening, they went to plays. 'This is wonderful,' Meg thought. 'I want to be rich. I hate being poor. It's terrible.'

One evening, the Moffats gave a party. Meg put on her old dress and her sash. She looked at the other girls' dresses. They were new and beautiful. Meg wasn't happy.

'They all know I'm poor,' she thought. Then some flowers arrived.

'They're for you, Meg!' cried the girls. 'Who are they from?'

'They're from Laurie and Mother,' said Meg. She was suddenly happier. She gave some flowers to the other girls. They put them in their hair or on their clothes.

Meg danced a lot that evening and enjoyed it very much. Then she heard two women talking.

'How old is that March girl?' said one woman.

'Sixteen or seventeen, I think,' said the other woman. It was Mrs Moffat.

'Did young Mr Laurence give her the flowers?'

'Yes. Mrs March must be very happy. A rich husband for her daughter to marry! That's a good plan.'

'The girl looks terrible. That dress! Maybe we can find her a better dress for the big party on Thursday?'

'And let's ask Mr Laurence to the party too!'

Meg's face was red as she listened. She was angry and sad. That night she didn't sleep.

* * *

Soon Thursday arrived. It was the day of the big party.

'What are you going to wear for the party?' Sallie asked Meg.

'My old white dress again,' said Meg. 'It's got a hole in it but it's the only one I've got.'

Annie's sister, Belle, said, 'I have a lovely blue dress, Meg. You can wear it.'

'You're very kind, Belle,' said Meg, 'but my dress is fine.'

'No, please wear my dress,' said Belle, 'and let me do your hair and face.' She smiled at Meg. 'You're going to be very beautiful.'

Meg just said thank you.

So that evening, Belle helped Meg to dress and did her hair and her face. Then she put some flowers in her dress and gave her a special handkerchief, a fan and a pair of high blue shoes.

'You are beautiful!' she said. Meg looked in the mirror. The new Meg was very, very different. She smiled.

At the party, everyone looked at Meg and talked about her. Lots of men asked her to dance.

Then Laurie arrived. Meg smiled and walked over to him.

'Jo wanted to know how you look,' said Laurie.

'And what are you going to tell her?' Meg asked.

'I'm going to say: 'I didn't know her!'' said Laurie. 'You're so different, Meg.'

'Don't you like me like this?'

'No,' said Laurie. 'You're not *you*! I like the old Meg.'

Meg walked away from Laurie. Behind her, someone said, 'What did they do to the March girl? They spoilt her!'

'Oh,' thought Meg, 'I was very stupid. My own clothes are lovely. I don't need to be another person.'

She went to find Laurie. 'Please don't tell Marmee and Jo about tonight,' she said. 'I'm going to talk to them.'

The next Saturday, Meg went home. That evening, she sat in the drawing room with her mother and Jo. She told them about her stay with the Moffats.

Suddenly she said, 'Oh, Marmee, I must tell you something.'

'What is it?' asked her mother.

Meg told them about the big party on Thursday. 'Belle Moffat dressed me and did my hair and face,' she said. 'At first I liked it. But then I knew it wasn't right for me!'

She told them too about Laurie and Mrs March's 'plans'.

Jo was very angry. 'That's not true!' she cried. 'Why didn't you tell them?'

But Marmee just said, 'I'm sorry, Meg. It wasn't a good idea for you to go.'

'Don't be sorry, Marmee,' said Meg. 'I'm going to forget all the bad things and only remember the good ones. But can I ask you something? Do you have 'plans' like Mrs Moffat said?'

'Yes, Meg, I have plans for my daughters,' said her mother. 'But I think my plans are very different from Mrs Moffat's. I want my daughters to be good, clever and happy and to help other people. And one day I hope you find a good man and make a home. Money is useful, but it's not everything. The most important thing is to be happy.'

CHAPTER 8
Secrets

Spring arrived, and then came summer. On June 1st, the holidays began.

The girls were so happy. Three months' holiday! Amy did drawings in the garden; Beth played the piano and learned some new music; Meg went shopping and bought pretty little things, and Jo read and went on the river in a boat with Laurie.

One day, Laurie asked the girls for lunch by the river. They all went up the river in two boats. Laurie, Jo and Beth went in one boat. Meg and Amy went in the other boat with Mr Brooke, Laurie's new tutor. Meg sat opposite Mr Brooke. She liked him. He was a quiet man, but he knew a lot of things. He was very good-looking and he had nice eyes. He looked at Meg a lot. Meg saw that. She smiled. When they arrived, everyone played games. Then they had lunch and coffee. Again, Meg sat with Mr Brooke. Mr Brooke had a German book.

'Oh, I'm not very good at German,' said Meg.

'I can help you,' said Mr Brook.

Meg read from the book. As she read, Mr Brooke watched her closely. He loved listening to her. He didn't care about her mistakes. 'That was wonderful!' he said.

* * *

Later that evening, Jo said to Meg, 'Did you have a good time today, Meg? You talked to Mr Brooke a lot.'

'Yes, I did,' said Meg. 'He's a very nice man. I like him very much.'

* * *

The holidays came to an end. Soon it was October again. The days were colder and the afternoons were short. Jo was at the top of the house. She finished the last page of her book. Then she wrote her name and put down her pen.

'The end!' she said.

She read it through once again. Then she put on her hat and coat. She walked quickly to the road and took a bus to town. She looked at the address on her paper. At last she found it and went in.

She was on her way home when she met Laurie.

'Jo! What are you doing in town?' he asked.

'Can you keep a secret?' she said.

'Of course!' said Laurie. 'I've got a secret for you too!'

'Well, I left two of my stories with a newspaper man,' she said. 'He's going to give me his answer next week.'

'Your stories are great, Jo!' cried Laurie. 'He's going to say yes.'

Jo laughed. 'I hope so,' she said. 'What's *your* secret?'

'Well ...' said Laurie, 'Meg left a glove at our house. Do you remember?'

'That's not a secret,' said Jo.

'No, but I saw it,' he said.

'Where did you see it?

'On Mr Brooke's desk.'

'No!'

'Yes. He loves her. Aren't you happy?'

'No, I'm not. Maybe he's going to take her away. I don't like the idea at all.'

For the next few weeks, Jo changed. Her sisters were surprised. She ran to the door every time the letters arrived. She often looked sadly at Meg. Then she ran and put her arms around her. She wasn't very nice to Mr Brooke. She had secret talks with Laurie all the time. She was a different person.

One day, Jo came into the parlour. She sat down and started to read the newspaper.

'What are you reading?' asked Meg.

'Just a story,' said Jo.

'Is it a good story?' asked Amy.

'Maybe you can read it to us,' said Beth.

So Jo read the story to her sisters. It was a very sad story. Most of the people in it died in the end. But it was a very good story.

'Who wrote it?' asked Beth.

Jo's face was red. 'Your sister did!' she said.

'You?' cried Meg.

'It's very good,' said Amy.

'I knew it!' said Beth. 'Oh, Jo! You're so clever!' Beth put her arms around Jo.

They all looked at the name in the newspaper: *Miss Josephine March*.

CHAPTER 9
Dark days

In November, a telegram arrived. Jo read it for everyone.

Mrs March.
Your husband is very ill. Please come at once.
S. HALE, Blank Hospital, Washington.

Mrs March was white. She sat down. 'I must go to Washington, children,' she said. 'I hope it isn't too late.'

They all started to cry. After a few minutes, Marmee said, 'I'm going to take the train tomorrow morning. I need some money for a doctor for Father. Laurie, can you take a letter to Aunt March?'

'Of course,' said Laurie.

'And girls, come and help me find my things.'

A little later, Mr Laurence and Mr Brooke arrived.

'I'm very sorry to hear about your father, Miss March,' Mr Brooke said to Meg. 'I came to tell you ... I can go with your mother to Washington.'

'That's very good of you, Mr Brooke,' Meg looked into his big brown eyes. 'Thank you very, very much.'

Jo went out. She came back an hour later. She put some money on the table.

'That's a lot of money, Jo!' said her mother. 'Where did you get it?'

Jo took off her hat. Her hair was short. 'Oh!' they all cried. 'Where's your beautiful long hair?'

'They gave me that money for it,' said Jo. 'I wanted to do something for Father. I don't care about my hair.'

In bed that night, Jo started to cry.

'Are you crying about Father, Jo?' asked Meg.

'No, not now.'

'What then?'

'My ... my hair!' cried Jo.

* * *

Before she left Mrs March spoke to the girls.

'Be good, do your work and please don't forget the Hummel family.'

'Yes, Marmee!' they cried.

Mrs March wrote letters often from Washington. Mr Brooke wrote every day too. Mr March was still ill, but he was much better. The girls started to feel happier.

Beth went every day to see the Hummels. One day, she asked Meg and Jo to go.

'Oh no, it's raining,' said Jo.

'And I'm tired,' said Meg. 'Why don't you go?'

'Because the baby is ill,' said Beth. 'I want you to see it.'

'Let's go tomorrow,' said Meg.

The next day, Beth looked terrible. Her eyes were red and she was very hot.

'Beth!' Jo cried. 'What is it?'

'I went to see the poor Hummel family,' said Beth. 'The youngest child was very ill. I tried to help him. But I was too late. He died in my arms. I think I'm ill too.'

'Oh no!' cried Jo. 'And Mother isn't here. We must call the doctor.'

The doctor came. He said Beth was very ill.

'We can't tell Mrs March,' said Hannah. 'She has enough problems now.'

Meg and Jo were very unhappy. They didn't listen to Beth when she needed them. Day after day, Jo sat by Beth's bed. Sometimes Beth didn't know her sisters. She called them different names. Sometimes Beth cried for her mother. Jo was frightened. They were dark and terrible days.

On the first of December, it snowed and the wind was cold. The doctor looked carefully at Beth. He took her hot hand. 'I think it's time to tell Mrs March,' he said. 'She needs to come home.'

'I'm going to write a telegram now,' said Jo.

They waited for mother to arrive. It was after two in the morning. Meg was by Beth's bed. Hannah sat in the chair. Her eyes were closed. Jo was at the window. Where was Marmee? Why didn't she come?

Suddenly, Meg moved. 'Oh no,' thought Jo. 'It's the end.'

She ran to the bed. Beth was different. She wasn't hot and red. She was white. Jo put her hand on Beth's face. 'Goodbye, my Beth, goodbye,' she said.

Hannah woke up and came to the bed. She looked at Beth and she listened. 'Oh!' she said. 'She's sleeping! She's going to be all right.'

Just then they heard the sound of a carriage. Marmee was home!

CHAPTER 10
Happy times

Beth slowly started to feel better. She moved from her bedroom to the drawing room. There she did her sewing and played with her cats. But she wasn't very strong. Jo took her around the house in her arms.

They had good news from Mr Brooke. Mr March was much better too. He hoped to come home early in the new year. 'It's going to be a very happy Christmas this year,' thought Jo.

On Christmas Day, Jo and Laurie took Beth to the window. There was a snow woman in the garden. She had a basket of fruit in one hand and some new music in the other. It was a present for Beth.

Beth laughed when she saw it. 'I'm so happy!' she said.

Jo opened her present. It was her favourite book. 'Me too,' she said.

'Oh, how lovely!' said Amy as she looked at her present: a beautiful painting.

'This is beautiful,' Meg said in her new dress. It was a present from Mr Laurence.

'I'm happy too,' said Mrs March. 'Now we only need your father.'

A little later, Laurie opened the parlour door. There was a very big smile on his face. He said, 'Here's another present for the March family.'

A tall man stood in the door. Mr Brooke helped him to walk.

'Father!'

Everyone got up quickly and ran to him. They put their arms around him. They laughed and they cried. They thanked Mr Brooke. They all talked at once. At last, Father was home.

Christmas dinner was very special that day. Mr Laurence, Laurie and Mr Brooke were there too. They enjoyed eating and drinking good things. They talked and laughed and told stories. After dinner, the family sat in front of the fire.

'Do you remember last year?' said Jo. 'We weren't very happy.'

'Christmas is very different this year,' said Beth.

'I can see some changes in my little women,' said their father.

'Oh tell us, Father!' said Meg.

'Well,' said Mr March, 'Meg's hands were white and pretty. Now they are red from work. But I think they are more beautiful now.'

'What about Jo?' asked Beth.

'Jo has short hair, but I see a young lady,' he said.

'Now Beth,' said Amy.

'She's not so shy,' he said. He looked at Amy. 'And Amy is not so spoilt. She thinks more about other people now.'

Their father was quiet for a moment and looked at his daughters. 'You are all lovely young women.'

CHAPTER 11
Meg decides

Meg wasn't Meg. She sat and dreamed all day. Every time she heard the name 'John Brooke', her face was red. Mr Brooke came often to the March's house. Mr and Mrs March didn't call him 'Mr Brooke' now. They called him John. Jo saw all this and she wasn't happy.

'Can I talk to you about something, Marmee?' she said one day.

'About Meg?'

'Yes! You're so clever, Marmee. How did you know?'

Her mother just smiled.

'Mr Brooke is poor,' said Jo. 'Don't you want a rich man for Meg?'

'Money is useful,' said her mother, 'but it's not everything. John is a good man. That's more important.'

'I want to keep Meg here,' said Jo.

'I know,' said her mother, 'but I think Meg loves John. And he loves her.'

Later, Jo and Meg were in the parlour.

'Mr Brooke is going to ask you to be his wife,' said Jo.

Meg smiled shyly. She liked the idea.

'What are you going to say to him?' asked Jo.

'Oh, Jo! I'm only sixteen,' said Meg.

'Please tell me what you are going to say.'

'I'm going to say this,' said Meg. ' "Thank you, Mr Brooke. I like you very much. But Mother and Father think I must wait. So please don't ask. Let's be friends like before." '

'That's very good,' said Jo. 'But are you going to say it?

They heard someone at the door. Meg looked down and started to sew very quickly. The door opened. It was Mr Brooke.

'Good afternoon,' he said. 'I came to see your father ...'

'I'm going to tell him,' said Jo. She ran out of the room.

Meg got up and started to move to the door too.

'Don't go, Margaret,' he said. 'Are you frightened of me?'

He called her Margaret for the first time. Meg's face was red. Mr Brooke took her hand.

'Oh no, please don't ...' said Meg.

'I only want to know something,' he said. 'Do you love me a little? I love you so much.'

'I don't know,' she said.

Suddenly, the door opened again. Aunt March came in. She was there to see Mr March.

'What's happening here?' she asked. Mr Brooke was very white. Meg was very red.

'Mr Brooke came to see father ...' Meg said.

Mr Brooke left the room quickly.

'Mr Cook?!' cried Aunt March. 'Laurie's tutor? I know about you two. What's he saying to you? Did you say yes? You need a rich husband and he has nothing. You aren't going to have my money if you're Mrs Cook!'

'Brooke!' Meg said. 'Not Cook!' She was very angry. And she suddenly decided.

'I'm going to be Mrs Brooke,' she said. 'I don't care about your money! Give it to the poor!'

Aunt March was angry too. 'You're not going to have anything from me,' she cried. 'I don't want to see you again. Goodbye!' She left and closed the door with a loud 'Bang'!

Fifteen minutes later, Jo came into the room. Meg was in Mr Brooke's arms!

'Oh no!' thought Jo. 'I don't believe it!'

Mr Brooke came across the room to her. 'Sister Jo!' he said. Jo didn't wait to hear more. She ran from the room.

That afternoon, Mr Brooke talked to Mr and Mrs March for a long time. That evening, he walked into dinner with Meg. They were both very, very happy.

After dinner, they all went into the parlour. Jo talked quietly to Laurie. 'I'm happy for Meg,' she said, 'but I don't want her to leave. She's my sister *and* my friend.'

'You've got me, Jo,' said Laurie. 'I'm your friend too. I'm always going to be your friend.'

'I know, Laurie,' she said. 'Thank you. It's true that everyone is very happy.'

Jo looked around the room. Father and Mother talked together. Amy drew a picture of Meg and John. Beth talked to Mr Laurence about music. And her good friend, Laurie was next to her. They were a very lucky family, she thought.

EPILOGUE

What happens next? Louisa May Alcott wrote a second book 'Good Wives'. This book tells us the next part of the story.

Meg marries John Brooke. They don't have a lot of money. They don't have a lot of pretty things. They live in a little house. They have some problems, but they are very happy. They have two children, a boy, Demi, and a girl, Daisy.

Jo writes more and more stories. One day, Laurie tells her he loves her. Jo loves Laurie, but as a friend. She feels sad. She goes away to New York. She writes, and works as a governess. In New York, she meets Professor Bhaer. Later, she marries him and they have a school for boys.

Beth was never very strong. She almost died when her mother was in Washington. As time goes by, she is often ill. She isn't very strong. She knows she is going to die. Jo and Marmee know it too. Sadly, Beth dies. Of course, her family never forget her.

Amy goes to Europe with her Aunt Carroll. They go to England, France and Italy. Amy sees many famous pictures. She does a lot of drawings. In France, she meets Laurie. They enjoy talking and being together. One day, Laurie asks Amy to marry him. She says yes.

Louisa May Alcott

Louisa May Alcott wrote *Little Women* in 1868. She was 36 years old and she wrote it in two and a half months! It was a big success.

Louisa May Alcott

Was *Little Women* a book for children?

Yes, it was a book for children, but older people read it too! Her readers loved it. They asked her to write another book. So in 1869, she wrote *Good Wives*. That was a big success too. In 1871 and 1886, Alcott wrote two more books: *Little Men* and *Jo's Boys*.

Where did the idea come from?

In some ways, Louisa Alcott's own life and family was the same as the March's in *Little Women*. Like Jo in the book, she lived in a house in Massachusetts and she had three sisters. Her family was poor and their life was very much like the March's. Like Jo, Alcott worked as a governess and as a writer. Like Jo, she was also a rebel.

But Alcott's life was different too. Alcott never married. And Alcott's father didn't go to war like Jo's father. He was against war. Alcott did more in the war than her father. She worked in a hospital.

Winona Ryder (Jo) and Christian Bale (Laurie) in the film of *Little Women*.

Why didn't Jo marry Laurie?

After the first book, readers asked Alcott: "Please can Jo marry Laurie in the next book?"

Alcott didn't want Jo to marry at all! She said no! But in the end, Jo married. She didn't marry Laurie. She married Professor Bhaer.

What other children's books were there at this time?

Lewis Carroll wrote *Alice in Wonderland* in 1865, Mark Twain wrote *Tom Sawyer* in 1876 and Robert Louis Stevenson wrote *Treasure Island* in 1884. All these books are still very popular and you can read them in many different languages.

What famous books were there at this time in your country? What were they about?

Is there a film of *Little Women*?
There isn't just one film ... there are more than ten films! The first film was in 1917. The last film was in 1994 and it had lots of stars in it – Winona Ryder (Jo), Claire Danes (Beth), Kirsten Dunst (Amy), Trini Alvarado (Meg), Christian Bale (Laurie) and Susan Sarandon (Marmee). There was also an opera in 1998 and a Broadway musical in 2005. The book, *Little Women* was very popular in Japan so there are some anime films of it too!

What do these words mean? You can use a dictionary.

success   rebel   play   opera   musical   popular

The American Civil War

The story of *Little Women* is at the time of the American Civil War (1861–1865). The Civil War was the most terrible war in America. Over 600,000 Americans died.

Slavery

In the 1850s, in the southern states of America, many white families had black slaves. There were four million slaves in America. They had a terrible life and many of them died young. People in the northern states didn't have slaves. They were against slavery.

Slaves working

Abraham Lincoln

North and south

In 1860, America had a new president. His name was Abraham Lincoln. He was against slavery. The eleven states in the south were frightened. They knew Lincoln wanted to stop slavery. They decided to break away from the northern states. They wanted to be a new country. On 12th April, 1861, the Civil War started. The southern states were the *Confederacy*. The northern states were the *Union*.

Not many doctors

Many women worked in the war hospitals. Louisa May Alcott was one of them. It wasn't an easy job. At the start of the war, the south only had twenty-four doctors. By 1865, there were many more doctors. There were 4,000 in the south and 13,000 in the north. Hospitals weren't always very clean and food and water were sometimes dirty. Many men died because of this.

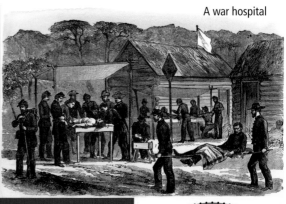
A war hospital

At the end of the war, many people's lives were very different. How, do you think?

The end of the war

The Civil War ended on 9th April, 1865. It was a victory for Abraham Lincoln and the northern states. A few days later, on 14th April, Lincoln was at a play in Washington with his wife and some friends. As he watched the play, a man called John Wilkes Booth from the southern states came up behind him. He shot Lincoln in the back of the head. It was a very sad day for America. But America was one strong country again. And it was the end of slavery.

Western territories

Oregon

California

☐ The Union   ▨ The Confederacy

What do these words mean? You can use a dictionary.

north / northern   president   shoot / shot   slave / slavery
south / southern   state   victory

51

Women in

When we read *Little Women*, we learn a lot about life in America in the 1800s. Things were different then for everyone, but they were very different for girls and women.

The man was the head of the family.

Life for women ...

In the 1800s, women usually stayed at home. They cleaned the house and cooked and sewed. They didn't often go out to work and many girls didn't go to school.

Women from very poor families worked as servants. Women from families like the March family in *Little Women* sometimes worked as governesses. There weren't any other jobs for women! The Civil War started to change things. Hospitals needed women. For the first time men saw that women were useful! Later, there were women doctors. Slowly, other jobs were possible too.

... and life for men

The man was the head of the family in those days. It was his job to give his family a home, food and clothes. His wife and children belonged to him. His wife's money and all her things belonged to him too!

the 1800s

Tennis and skating

Women had big, long dresses in the 1800s so it was difficult to play sports. It wasn't possible for them to wear trousers in those days. Some women skated or played tennis in their long skirts, but it wasn't easy.

There were no sports for women at the first Olympic Games in Athens in 1896. In 1900, there were just two sports open to women: tennis and golf.

No school for girls!

Girls in the 1800s didn't need to learn important things because women stayed at home. Not many girls went to school. No women went to university. Universities were for men only. The University of Iowa was the first American university to open its doors to women in 1855. The first English university was the University of London in 1878.

The vote

At the time of *Little Women*, women didn't vote. The first country to give women the vote was New Zealand, in 1893. In the United States, it was 1920. In Britain, it was 1928. And in Switzerland, it was only in 1971.

> When did women first vote in your country? What do you think was the best thing about living in the 1800s? What was the worst?

> **What do these words mean?**
> **You can use a dictionary.**
> belong   golf   servant   tennis
> university   vote

CHAPTERS 1–4

Before you read

1 Match a word in A with a word in B. You can use your dictionary.

A	B
act shy Christmas skate	ice lady play present

2 Complete the sentences with these words. You can use your dictionary.

hole   spoilt   War   whistle   perfume   pencil

a) Some people can … very loudly, but I can't!

b) Her parents give her everything she wants. She's so …

c) The Second World … ended in 1945.

d) I want to draw a picture. I need some paper and a …

e) There's a big … in my trousers! I can't go out like this!

f) I bought some expensive … for my mum on her birthday.

3 Look at 'People and Places' on pages 4–5. Answer these questions.

a) Who is away from his / her family? Why?

b) Which sister isn't a teenager yet?

c) Which sister enjoys writing?

d) Which sister doesn't talk much?

After you read

4 Answer the questions about Christmas presents.

a) Why weren't there many presents for the March family this year?

b) What presents did they buy for their mother?

c) What present did the March family give Mrs Hummel and her children?

d) What present did Mr Laurence give the March family?

5 Who said this? Who did they say it to?

a) 'My dress has a big hole in the back.'

b) 'You must have gloves!'

c) 'Have you got nice handkerchiefs?'

d) 'I lived in Europe for many years.'

6 Match the two columns.
   a) Meg   i) was old and needed someone to help her.
   b) Jo   ii) told her daughters a clever story.
   c) Beth   iii) went to school and had a lot of friends.
   d) Amy   iv) didn't enjoy working for her aunt.
   e) Mrs March   v) was a governess for a rich family.
   f) Aunt March vi) stayed at home and helped in the house.

7 What do you think?
   Which sister would you like to be ... most? ... least? Why?

CHAPTERS 5–8

Before you read
8 Complete the sentences with these words. You can use your dictionary.
   ill   marry   flowers   river   secret   snow
   a) It's very cold and the sky is white. I think it's going to ...
   b) Please don't tell anyone. It's a ...
   c) You're very hot and you look terrible! I think you're ...
   d) What's the longest ... in the world? Is it the Mississippi?
   e) You can't ... your boyfriend! You're only ten!
   f) The ... in your garden are beautiful.

9 What do you think?
   Look at the titles of Chapters 5 and 6. Who is going to make friends in 'Making friends' and what is the terrible thing in 'A terrible thing to do'?

After you read
10 Put these parts of the story in order.
   a) Jo met Laurie's grandfather.
   b) Laurie played games with the March girls at their house.
   c) Jo saw Laurie in his bedroom window.
   d) Beth went to the Laurence house to play the piano.
   e) Jo went to visit Laurie.

11 Choose the correct words.

    a) Amy went / didn't go to the play with Meg, Jo and Laurie.

    b) Amy put Jo's book / dress on the fire.

    c) Jo was very angry / pleased with Amy.

    d) The ice in the centre of the river was / wasn't strong.

    e) Amy / Laurie went into the icy water.

    f) Jo and Amy were / weren't friends again later that day.

12 Answer the questions.

    a) What differences were there between the March family and the Moffat family?

    b) What did Meg wear for the two parties? What did Laurie think of her at the big party?

    c) What different plans did Mrs March and Mrs Moffat have for their daughters?

13 What do you think?

    What do you wear to a party? How are parties different now?

CHAPTER 9 – Epilogue

Before you read

14 What do you think?

    Look at the titles of the next chapters. What do you think is going to happen in 'Dark days' and 'Happy times'? In 'Meg decides', what is Meg going to decide?

After you read

15 Are these sentences right or wrong?

    a) Mrs March went alone to Washington.

    b) It was easy for Jo to sell her hair: she didn't care about it.

    c) Beth was very ill after she visited the Hummel family.

    d) Mr March arrived home on Christmas Day.

    e) Meg decided to marry Mr Brooke before Aunt March arrived.

16 What do you think?

    Do you like the Epilogue? Do you want to change any parts of it?